Modern Curriculum Press

**BEGINNING
TO
READ**
Series

Help for Dear Dragon

Margaret Hillert

Illustrated by David Helton

ISBN: 0-8136-5631-1
Printed in the United States of America

23 24 25 26 27   06 05

1-800-321-3106
www.pearsonlearning.com

Here you are.

Here is something to eat.

It is what you like.

DRAGON

No?
You do not want it?
That is funny.

You did not want to get up.
Now you do not want to eat.
You do not look good.
What is it?
What can I do?

You are not happy.
I am not happy.
This is not good.
I have to get help for you.

Come on now.

Get in here.

We will go for help.

9

Away we go.
This way.
This way.
You will see.

11

Here it is.

This is where we want to go.
In here. In here.

Oh, my.
Look here —
      and here —
            and here.

14

Have you come to
get help, too?
This is a good
spot for it.

Come in.

Come in.

Jump up here.

I want to have a look at you.

I will look down here to
see what I can see.

Oh, oh.

My, you do not look
too good.
Not too good, but I
can help.

I want to look at this, too.
I want to find out something
with this.

Now I will do this.
This will be a big
help to you.

Yes, yes.
This is good for you.
And you are a good
little dragon.

Here is something red.
I want you to have this too.
It is something that will help.

Now you can get down.
Down,
    down,
        down.

PET DOCTOR
DR. LEE
D. V. M.

And away you go.
You will want to eat now.
You will want to
run and play.

Come on. Come on.
Run, run, run.
I will get you something
good to eat.

Here you are.
Eat it up, and we will
go out to play.
What fun we will have!

Here you are with me.
And here I am with you.
Now it is a happy day, dear dragon.

Margaret Hillert, author and poet, has written many books for young readers. She is a former first-grade teacher and lives in Birmingham, Michigan.

Help for Dear Dragon uses the 67 words listed below.

a	find	like	something
all	for	little	spot
am	fun	look	
and	funny		that
are		me	this
at	get	my	to
away	go		too
	good	no	
be		not	up
big	happy	now	
but	have		want
	help	oh	way
can	here	on	we
come	how	out	what
			where
day	I	play	will
dear	in		with
did	is	red	
do	it	run	yes
down			you
dragon	jump	see	
eat			